CANTICLE OF THE ROSE

EIGHT PIECES FOR ORGAN
BY ALAN RIDOUT

We hope you enjoy the music in *Canticle of the Rose*. Further copies are available from your local music or christian bookshop.

In case of difficulty, please contact the publisher
direct by writing to:

The Sales Department
KEVIN MAYHEW LTD
Rattlesden
Bury St Edmunds
Suffolk IP30 0SZ

Phone 0449 737978
Fax 0449 737834

Please ask for our complete catalogue of outstanding Church Music.

Canticle of the Rose is recorded on *A Crown of Light.*
Lammas Records, compact disk LAMM078D.

First Published in Great Britain in 1992 by
KEVIN MAYHEW LTD
Rattlesden
Bury St Edmunds
Suffolk IP30 0SZ

© Copyright 1992 by Kevin Mayhew Ltd

ISBN 0 86209 236 1

Cover design, based on the Rose window in St Albans Cathedral, Hertfordshire, by Juliette Clarke
Printed and bound in Great Britain by
J. B. Offset Printers (Marks Tey) Limited

Contents

Foreword

The eight movements in this work, whose title was suggested by a poem of Edith Sitwell, were inspired by the Rose Window in St Alban's Cathedral, Hertfordshire, England, and they are directly related to the symbolism of the window. The three movements, Father, Son and Spirit were first played at the Service of Dedication and Thanksgiving on the occasion of the unveiling of the Rose Window in the presence of HRH Princess of Wales on September 26 1989, and the fanfare which concludes the final movement was played at the moment of unveiling.

The work may be played as a cycle, as separate items, or in one of two suggested suites: a) Earth, Fire, Air, Water and Postlude, or b) Father, Son, Spirit and Postlude. The total duration is approximately 24 minutes.

About the Composer

Alan Ridout (b. 1934) is one of England's most prolific composers, producing a steady stream of works in most forms: symphonies, operas, ballet music, chamber music, song cycles and church music.

He studied with Gordon Jacob and Herbert Howells at the Royal College of Music and later with Peter Racine Fricker, Michael Tippett, and the Dutch composer Henk Badings. He has taught at four universities, including Oxford and Cambridge, and for over twenty years was also a professor at the Royal College of Music.

Kevin Mayhew publishes much of Alan Ridout's choral and organ music and the following books are edited and arranged by him:

The Organist's Library – a series of books containing music for manuals.

The Organist's Collection – a series of books containing music for manuals and pedals.

CANTICLE OF THE ROSE
Alan Ridout

I EARTH

7

II Father

III FIRE

Presto (♩ = c. 160)

IV SON

V Air

VI SPIRIT

27

VII WATER

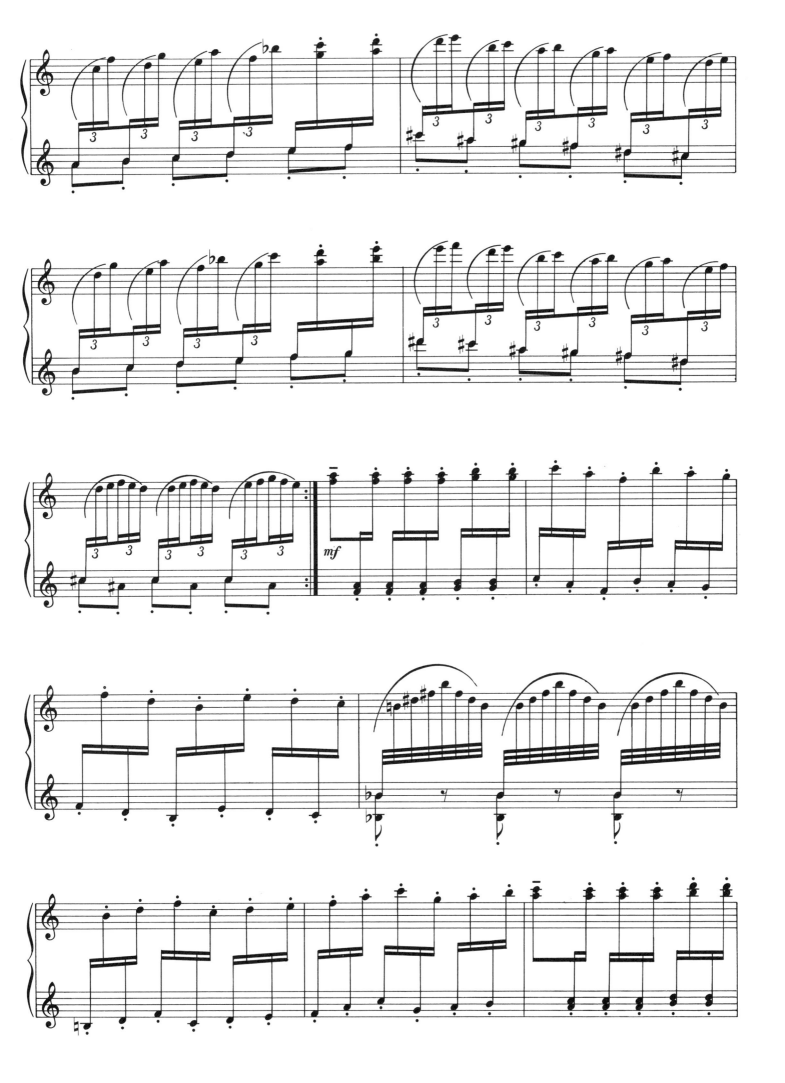

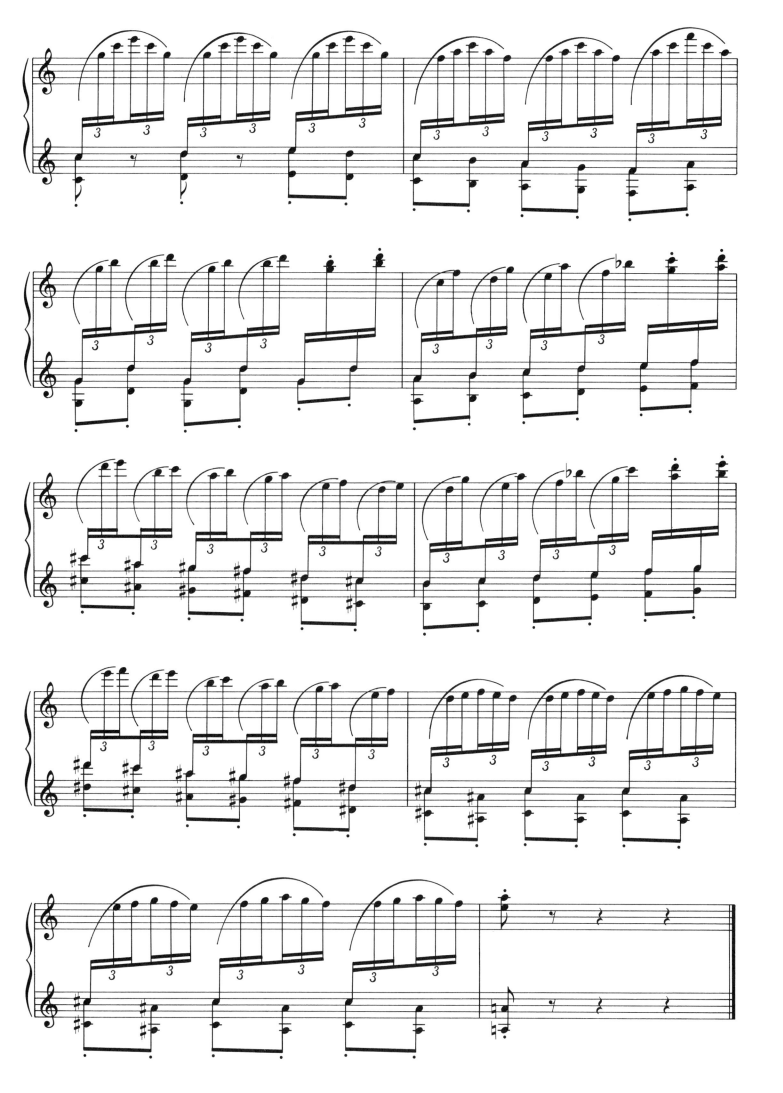

VIII POSTLUDE (VARIANTS)

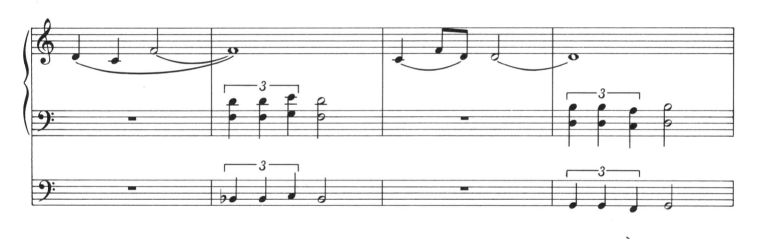

IV Rubato